Contents

"Rhonda Parrish is a shapeshifter with talents to match her every incarnation- magpie tenacity for picking the shiniest submissions, nightingale notes for crafting tales, and bright, feline eyes for seeking out her photographic subjects. She balances on the knife-edge of darkness and light, a sorceress of both realms."

—Sara Cleto

Praise for White Noise:

"A collection of vivid scenes laid out in sharp and articulate verse, that when assembled, construct a grim narrative filled with tension, stark imagery, and unusual beauty. WHITE NOISE reaches in and evokes a visceral response— not always the one you'd expect."

—Tim Deal, Shroud Quarterly

"In this collection of poems, Rhonda Parrish manages to capture all the emotions of life during an apocalypse: From fear and desperation to pain and sorrow. She even shows us love and hope. Some serious but most tinged with humor. This is a great collection of poems about the zombie apocalypse."

—Carol Hightshoe - author of the Chaos Reigns Saga and Editor of Zombiefied I, II and III

White Noise

Poems of the Zombie Apocalypse

Rhonda Parrish

White Noise - Poems of the Zombie Apocalypse

Copyright © 2014 Rhonda Parrish
Published by Poise and Pen Publishing
2014

ISBN: 978-0-9936990-3-0 (physical)
ISBN: 978-1-988233-78-9 (electronic)

http://www.poiseandpen.com

Cover Design by James, GoOnWrite.com

Datura stramonium

Swallow it down, swallow it down
Down the rabbit hole you go,
Join the hatter, sup the tea,
Swallow it down.

The flowers they beckon you
Virgin white, soft as a horse's nose
But the pods, they bite.
Beware the bite, but swallow it down

Something is fucked up man,
When reality is too surreal to be real
When the fog makes more sense
The rabbit hole.
Beware the bite

Different here, no teeth, just thorns
Angry thorns, feather-soft petals,
The weed will take you, wrap you in sound
You don't need to see, listen to the light
Block out the sights

The screams are surely phantoms
Summoned from fraudulent memories
The shuffle, the moans, bury them deep
Stuff them down the hole.
Close your eyes

Surrender to the fog.
Swallow it down.
The pain, the truth, the reality.
Beware the bite.

Genesis

The water lapped at her
tugging the tension from her body
pulling it out to sea.

The moon watched
leaving a long white trail on the surface
bleeding toward the horizon.

She swam
naked.
It's not safe, he'd said, but she'd laughed.

She thought it was weeds
winding around her calf
as, refreshed, she walked through the shallows
toward shore.

Too late she realised it was fingers.

Then teeth.

One gave way,
pushed from rotting gums as the thing
bit her.
She felt it bend beneath her flesh then,
impossibly, heard it splash into the water
while a fear-gorged scream
wrestled free of her throat

She tumbled into the surf and
kicked at the thing,
felt what might have been a nose
crumple beneath her heel

Free, she stumbled
gasping,
like a beached fish
on the damp sand

but it was too late.

Her blood stained her skin in the moonlight,
pumping out to paint the sand.
It's not safe, he'd said, but she'd laughed,
asked,
What harm could it do?

When The Screaming Stopped

Darkness clawed across her eyes
on spider's legs
and numbness stole over her.

Peace
for a moment
then a flicker, a flare of awareness
sparked deep within

She tried to bury it,
to enjoy the absence of pain
the embrace of death
but it was persistent.

Like a pit bull
or the infected that had claimed her
it wouldn't let go.

Her lids snapped open
She sniffed the air
Only one thing mattered now
Flesh
Warm and willing.

It was out there somewhere
as she had been,
like chicken on the barbeque
ready to be turned.

Breakfast in Bed

If I'd woken you
instead of sneaking out of bed
and running to the Tim Horton's
so I could surprise you with your favourite.
You wouldn't have been here
when they came
and you'd be looking at a bagel
the way you're looking at me now.

Last Thoughts

Scrawled in blood
across the wall
"I never told her"

Slippery When Wet

Hiding behind the counter
of the 7-11
Ann heard Gary scream
then the wet, gurgling sound
so familiar these days
and swallowed her fist to silence herself.

The sounds of feeding ended
consumed by the shuffling steps
of hungry undead.
Two now.

A whimper escaped her
on the heels of a hiccup.
The shambling paused. Turned.
Gained speed as it approached.

She bolted from the counter
darting out like a deer from a ditch—
right into what used to be Gary.

They pinballed away from each other
he ricocheted off an empty shelf
that used to hold Doritos
she bounced down the aisle for cleaning supplies.

She righted herself, regained her footing,
sprinted toward the door.

She was going to make it!
Then rounding the corner
her heel connected with the pool of Gary's blood.
She dropped like a sandbag
and felt something snap.

Maybe Not

The revolver held six bullets.
The minister had claimed one
The thing that had once been her daughter two —
her hand shook.
Her husband had been easier,
one shot.
Had Nanna taken one, or two?
She couldn't remember.
Mom, dad and granddad were coming now,
she could hear them at the door.
She tasted the metal and the oil,
the bitter tang of gunpowder.
Was there a shot left?
Maybe...

White Noise

Every station
ran the same thing
over and over
"This is not a test!"
All but one.

A Christian station
Sermons interspersed with donation calls
twenty four hours a day.

An atheist, she still listened
if only to hear a human voice
express an emotion
other than fear.

Still, looking out at the
shambling masses that filled the street
she had to chuckle when the preacher
offered up eternal life
as some sort of reward.

The Hardest Promise I Ever Kept

"If I'm being kept alive through artificial means,"
she'd said, squeezing my hand so tight
I could feel the bones grinding together.
"Promise me you'll pull the plug."

Today, my fingers shake and tears blur my vision
But I'll do what I promised and pull it,
not the plug, but the trigger.

Attachment

It's what dogs do,
sniffing out dead meat,
rolling in it, eating it...

had I thought about it I'd have known
but then, in those early days
I had bigger things on my mind...

Now they're out there,
obscene imitations of what they used to be
like the shamblers, I suppose.
But the dogs...
They break my heart like the people don't.
Their wild eyes, drooling mouths.
I cry when I shoot them...

Cry in a way I haven't for people in a
very long time.
I cry, and pray I never see mine.

Should I Die...

The bed, soft, embracing
down-filled comforter of the purest white
stark in its cleanliness.
A mirror at its head reflects my face
Blood-spattered, dark with dirt
and the ashes of so many fires.
My hair is brushed
but filthy.
The water stopped running weeks ago.
Biting my lip, I taste salt, and iron.
The bed tempts me, beckons me but
I grab my sleeping bag
roll it out on the floor
while the prayer from my childhood
sing-songs through my mind.
Now I lay me down to sleep...

Hunger

The juices, sweet and reddish brown, trickled
across her fingers, ran in rivulets across her hands,
dripped down her chin

Frenzied, she grunted unintelligibly while
she scooped up handfuls and shoveled them into
her gaping maw.

Not bothering to chew, the lumps slipped, whole,
Down her parched throat.
Dark and delicious.

She'd thought for sure she was going to die holed up in her house
would that be ironic?
To starve during the zombie apocalypse?

It didn't matter now.
Even the moans, growing nearer outside didn't matter
All that mattered were the beans.

The giant can of baked beans she'd discovered—
wedged in a corner of the stranger's pantry.
She fed.

The Bunker

It's an old bomb shelter in a hollowed-out hill
We hide here. Naked bulbs swing in narrow hallways
and tomb-like chambers, beneath more concrete than I like to
think about.
Two entrances (one for emergencies only)
with thick iron doors, two sets—like an airlock.
Guarded twenty four hours a day.
We've got stores here, enough to last for years
and grow-lights to offer hope for more.
But I've felt it, that itch, like bugs under your skin,
you just can't scratch.
The need to breathe, to get out, to be out there.
There, where they are.
I've seen it in the eyes of other people here.
Soledad is getting twitchy,
Mark mumbles under his breath and counts,
counts everything. Over and over again.
If Chloe says "Aren't we lucky?"
in her chipper valley girl voice one more time...

Cover Up

Sweat runs in torrents
Down Aaron's waxy grey face
Soaking his collar
Painting dark stripes under his arms
Down his back.
He trembles, teeth chattering
Hands rubbing the goosebumps
On his upper arms
"I'll be okay," he mutters
whenever anyone asks.
"It's just the flu,
really bad. Yes, I'm sure."
He knows before long one of them
Probably Annie, she's got the balls for it,
Will demand to search him,
Will find the bite
Black, rancid and swollen.
He knows,
As he huddles in the corner of his bed
Rocking back and forth in the darkness
That he's endangering them
That his life is over
But he can't find it in himself to be the hero.
He clings, desperately
To the vestiges of life he still possesses
Praying to whatever God might be listening
For a miracle.

Fluffy

A lame name, perhaps, but I wasn't feeling creative
that day when I found her, hiding under the porch
at MacPherson's old place. The same deck I ducked under
when I saw the shuffling mob coming down the street.
I'd seen her, a shadow within the shadows, her eyes
so wide open her iris was the thinnest band of gold;
like the ring Jo had given me, before this all started,
the one I lost trying to pull away from the shambler
the week before. She hissed, and arched her back,
not at me, but at the dirty feet, some shoeless, some
stumps, that marched past us out there.
I reached, with fingers shaking like the last leaf clinging
to the trees, and ran my hand down her back,
praying it would hush her, and not make her louder.
She pressed against me, rubbing my palm with her greasy fur,
a low rumble, like gargled gravel, emanating from her throat.
Purring.
It had been so long since I'd heard it, or any sound
reminiscent of joy. For it to be now, while the battered
battalion of undead dragged themselves by, made tears
creep into my eyes. Silent tears, thank God.
Now, as the snow blankets the ground, she rests
spread across my lap, vibrating gently, warming
my legs and my heart. The only other thing,
within hundreds of miles, perhaps,
with a heartbeat.

After the Storm

The snow glistened white, pure and sweet
the wind had blown, thawing the top layer
that it might freeze again, a thin crust
like the sugar upon a creme brulee.
She'd never learned to walk, it seemed
and it was too late to master the trick
Her grey fingers, pudgy with dimpled knuckles,
splayed wide upon the ground and she crawled
inching forward, bit by bit.
Behind her, the thing that had been her mother
shambles forward through the snow to her knees
it trips her, and she tumbles forward
into the drift. Buried, flailing like a swimmer
going down for the third time.
But the infant continues on, little by little.
Her lips curled into a snarl
her stomach screaming with a hunger
no bottle can sate.

Beneath

Naked boughs
cast pallid shadows
across the snow
and Spring's breath reveals
twisted digits
curled into ashen claws
with the barest hint
of chipped red polish.

Obscured

Ghosts of the city
peer out of the gloom
around him
As a child he'd loved it
when the 'clouds fell down'
and cloaked his world
in mysteries
Now, though,
it was just one more thing
to hide the shamblers.
One more obstacle to
his survival.
One more enemy.

The Cleansing

Fire, insatiable and indiscriminate
consumes the streets
and the ghouls
too slow, too mindless, to run.
Cries of collapsing buildings
hollowed by flames and
as empty as the undead,
rise above the roar of the inferno;
a chorus of suffering

Loneliness

That tree, the crabapple, its trunk twisted and gnarly,
the V in its branches at just the right height—
I used to climb it. Before.
I'd sit in its crook, back pressed against the rough bark,
eyes devouring the words of Jane Austen, else turned up,
peering through the canopy, watching light dance over the green
as the wind ruffled the leaves.

Now, bent as an old man,
with one powerful limb torn off—splintered and bleeding sap,
its embrace would be too weak to support me.
Tenaciously, it continues to blossom. Even now, even still.
A hammering wind forces its way between the houses,
tearing the blushing pink blooms from its grip and scattering
them,
so many bits of confetti,
over the ashes that cover the ground like snow.

Acknowledgements

Maybe Not... was originally published by *Everyday Weirdness*, December 2009

Fluffy was originally published by *Daikaijuzine*, June 2010

White Noise was originally published by *Everyday Weirdness*, June 2010

Attachment was originally published by *Star*Line*, September 2010

After the Storm was originally published by T*ales from the Zombie War*, October 2010

Slippery When Wet was originally published by *Static Movement*, October 2010

Hunger was originally published in *Demonminds 2010 Halloween Edition*, October 2010

Last Thoughts was originally published in *Star*Line*, December 2010

Should I Die... was originally published in *Sex and Murder Magazine*, January 2011

Loneliness first appeared in *Golden Visions Magazine*, January 2011

Obscured was first published by *Bête Noire*, April 2011

Cover Up was first published by *Eclectic Flash*, September 2011

The Bunker was first published by *Dark Chaos*, October 2011

Genesis was first published by *Dark Chaos*, October 2011

Beneath was first published by *Every Day Poets*, February 2013

About the Poet

Like a magpie, **Rhonda Parrish** is constantly distracted by shiny things. She's the editor of many anthologies and author of plenty of books, stories and poems. She lives with her husband and three cats in Edmonton, Alberta, and she can often be found there playing Dungeons and Dragons, bingeing crime dramas or cheering on the Oilers.

Her website, updated regularly, is at http://www.rhondaparrish.com and her Patreon, updated even more regularly, is at https://www.patreon.com/RhondaParrish.

Although completely discordant on the surface, zombies and comedy complement one another immensely and have a long history of doing so. This collection of three funny zombie stories nods to that tradition and continues it.

Available now:

Waste Not (And Other Funny Zombie Stories)

Rhonda Parrish
Author, Editor and Hydra-slayer

If you enjoy this book please consider supporting my Patreon where, for as little as $1 a month you get:

- **Exclusive stories and poems you can't read anywhere else**

- **Behind-the-scenes access to make sure you are always 100% in the loop**

- **Early access to books, stories, cover reveals and inside information**

- **Books, stories and merch in your inbox and your mailbox**

And more!

Click here to access and for more information
(or copy/paste this into your browser →
https://www.patreon.com/RhondaParrish)

Always Be The First To Know!

Whether it's a new release, a call for submissions, cover reveal, super sale or I just want to share a new story I've written, you will always be among the first to know if you sign up for my newsletter.

I promise to respect your privacy and your inbox. I will only email you when I have something exciting to share, probably about twice a month.

Subscribe now and you'll receive a free download of my award-winning post-apocalyptic short story, "Starry Night" as a welcome-to-the-newsletter present!

Subscribe to Rhonda's Mailing List!

http://bit.ly/StarryStory

ALSO BY RHONDA PARRISH

Written by

APHANASIAN STORIES

WASTE NOT (AND OTHER FUNNY ZOMBIE STORIES)
WHITE NOISE: POETRY OF THE ZOMBIE APOCALYPSE
THE OTHER SIDE OF THE DOOR

HOLLOW

EERIE EDMONTON
HAUNTED HOSPITALS

RHONDA PARRISH ANTHOLOGIES

Available Now

A IS FOR APOCALYPSE

B IS FOR BROKEN

C IS FOR CHIMERA

D IS FOR DINOSAUR

E IS FOR EVIL

F IS FOR FAIRY

FAE

CORVIDAE

SCARECROW

SIRENS

EQUUS

MRS. CLAUS: NOT THE FAIRY TALE THEY SAY

TESSERACTS TWENTY-ONE: NEVERTHELESS

METASTASIS

NITEBLADE MAGAZINE

FIRE: DEMONS, DRAGONS AND DJINNS

EARTH: GIANTS, GOLEMS AND GARGOYLES

AIR: SYLPHS, SPIRITS AND SWAN MAIDENS

GRIMM, GRIT AND GASOLINE

CLOCKWORK, CURSES AND COAL

HEAR ME ROAR

SWASHBUCKLING CATS: NINE LIVES ON THE SEVEN SEAS

www.ingramcontent.com/pod-product-compliance
Lightning Source LLC
Chambersburg PA
CBHW020322150626
46552CB00022B/3156